This Walker Book belongs to:

_____

_____

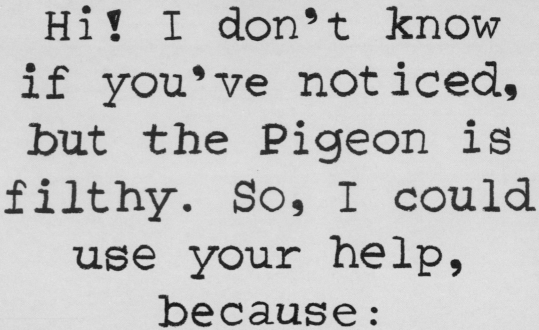

Hi! I don't know if you've noticed, but the Pigeon is filthy. So, I could use your help, because:

First published in Great Britain 2014 by Walker Books Ltd
87 Vauxhall Walk, London SE11 5HJ

First published in the United States 2014 by Hyperion Books for Children, an imprint of Disney Book Group. British publication rights arranged with Wernick & Pratt Agency, LLC.

10 9 8 7 6 5 4 3 2 1

Copyright © 2014 Mo Willems

The right of Mo Willems to be identified as author/illustrator of this work has been asserted by him in accordance with the Copyright, Designs and Patents Act 1988.

This book has been handlettered by Mo Willems

Printed in Singapore

British Library Cataloguing in Publication Data: a catalogue record for this book is available from the British Library.

ISBN 978-1-4063-5778-3

www.walker.co.uk
www.pigeonpresents.com

The Pigeon Needs a Bath!

words and pictures by mo willems

WALKER BOOKS
AND SUBSIDIARIES
LONDON · BOSTON · SYDNEY · AUCKLAND

That is a matter of opinion.

to Cher, who always
makes a splash

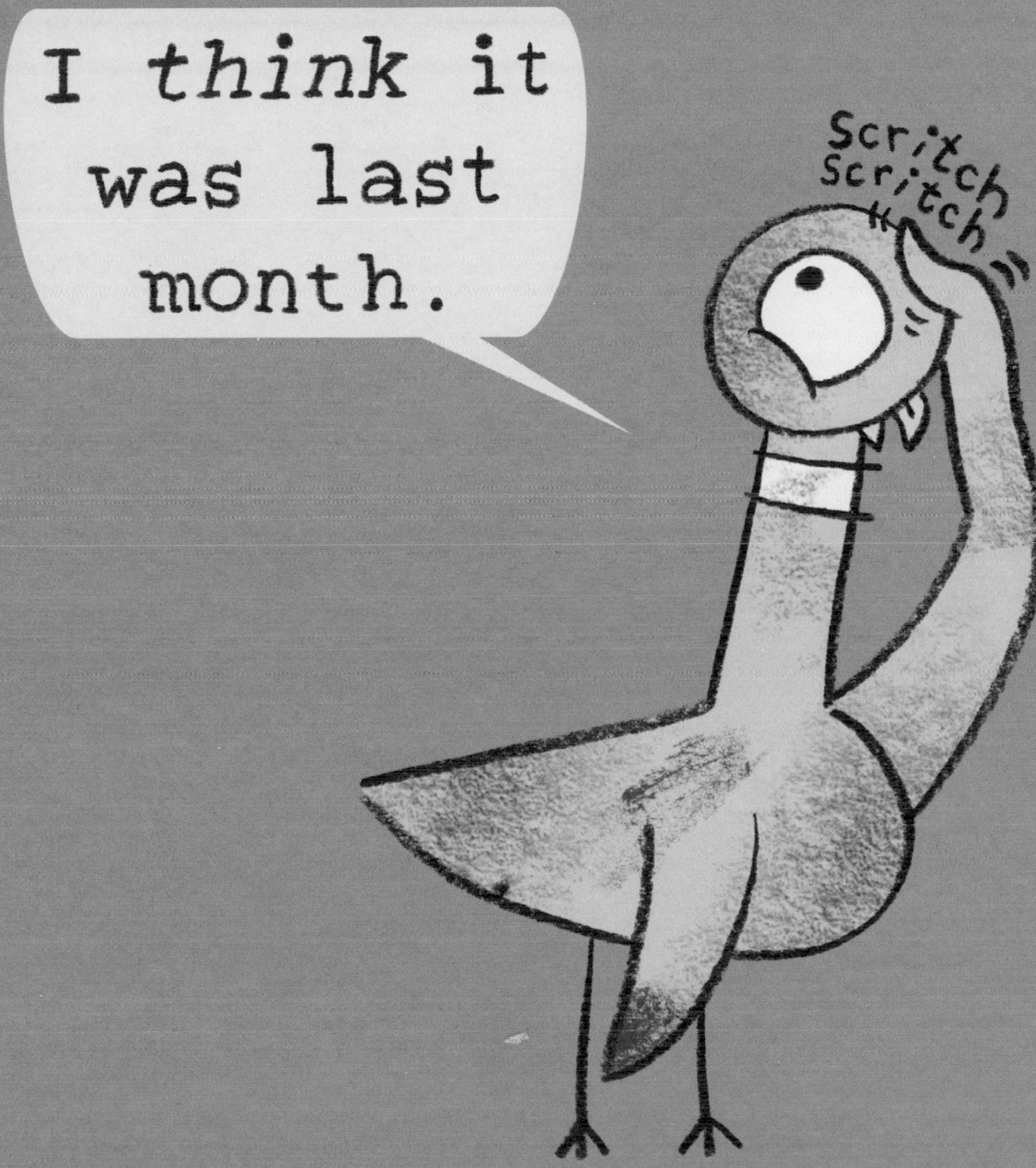
I think it was last month.
Scritch Scritch

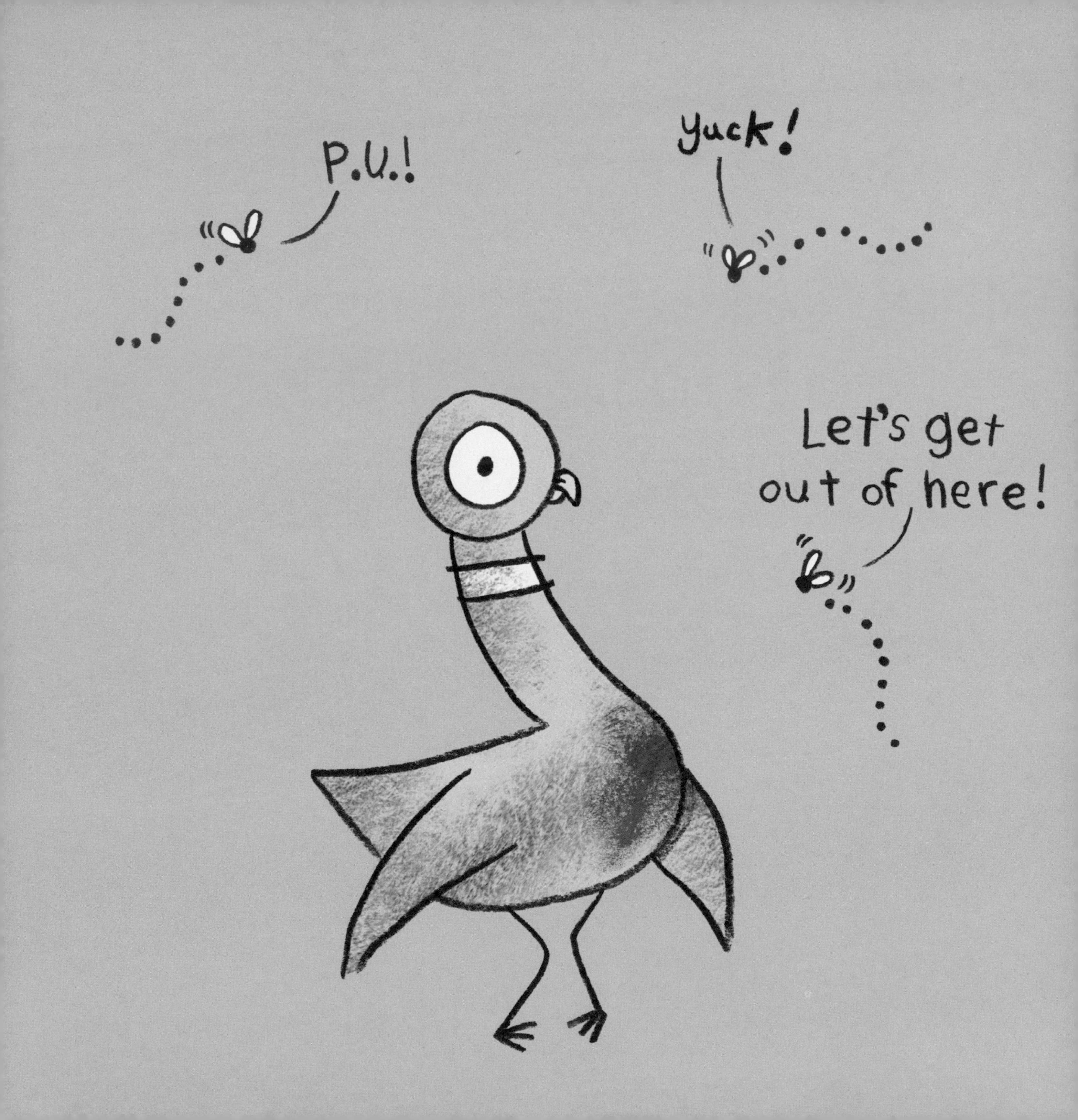
P.U.!
Yuck!
Let's get out of here!

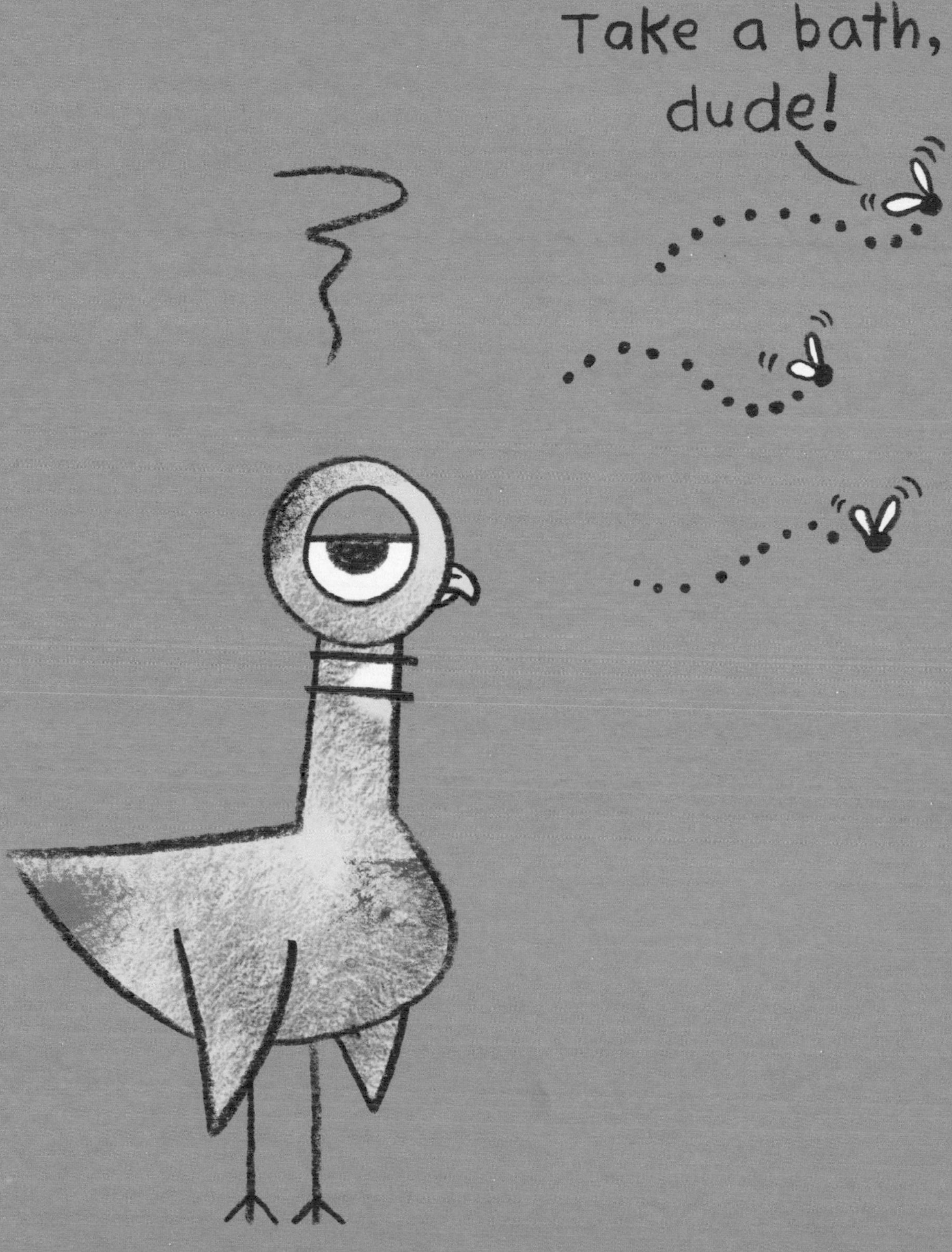
Take a bath, dude!

Item(s) reserved.

Current time: 16/11/2021,
14:31
Item ID: C901648901
Title: Tiddler
Author: Donaldson, Julia,
User ID 1002020619
User name: Mrs Sara
Gribben
Pickup By: 26/11/2021

LibrariesNi

TEN HOURS LATER

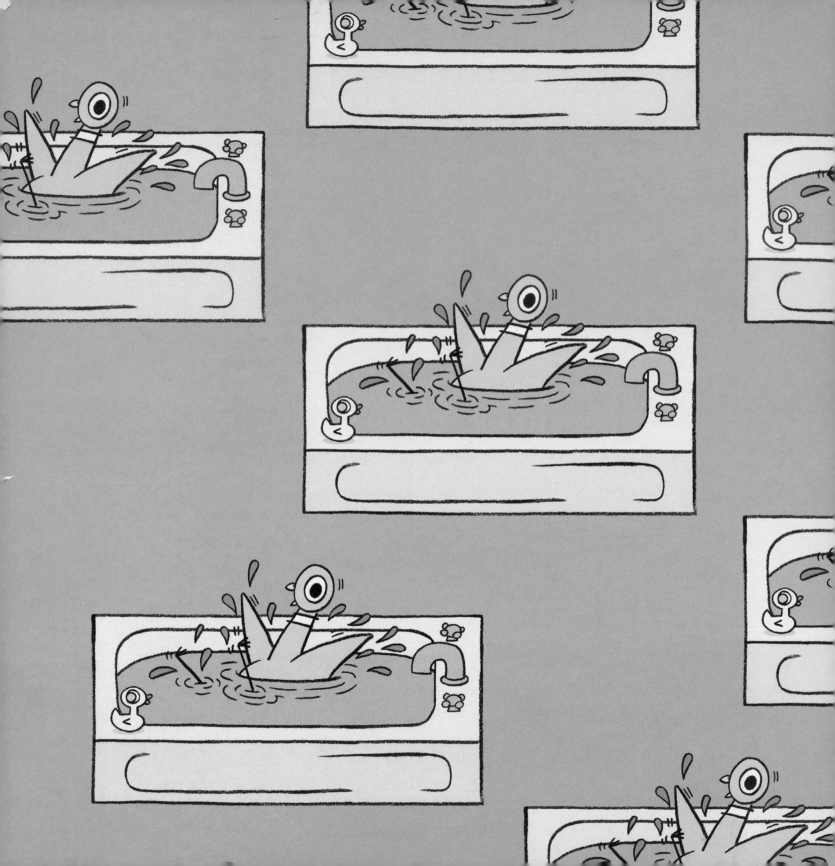

Other books by MO WILLEMS

The Pigeon Finds a Hot Dog!

words and pictures by mo willems

ISBN: 978-1-8442-8545-7

Don't Let the Pigeon Stay Up Late!

words and pictures by mo willems

ISBN: 978-1-4063-0812-9

Don't Let the Pigeon Drive the Bus!

words and pictures by mo willems

ISBN: 978-1-8442-8513-6

The Pigeon Wants a Puppy!

I really do!

words and pictures by mo willems

ISBN: 978-1-4063-1550-9

The Duckling Gets a Cookie!?

words and pictures by mo willems

ISBN: 978-1-4063-4009-9

Don't Let the Pigeon Finish This Activity Book!

More than 250 pages of GAMES, EVENTS and HOT DOGS!

A superfun book by mo willems and YOU!

ISBN: 978-1-4063-4731-9

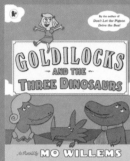

GOLDILOCKS AND THE THREE DINOSAURS

As Retold by MO WILLEMS

ISBN: 978-1-4063-5532-1

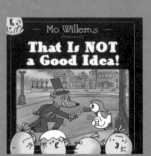

Mo Willems Presents That Is NOT a Good Idea!

ISBN: 978-1-4063-4941-2

KNUFFLE BUNNY

A CAUTIONARY TALE BY Mo Willems

ISBN: 978-1-8442-8059-9

KNUFFLE BUNNY TOO

A CASE OF MISTAKEN IDENTITY BY Mo Willems

ISBN: 978-1-4063-1382-6

KNUFFLE BUNNY FREE

AN UNEXPECTED DIVERSION BY Mo Willems

ISBN: 978-1-4063-3649-8

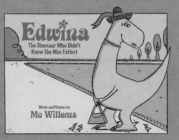

Edwina
The Dinosaur Who Didn't Know She Was Extinct

Words and Pictures by Mo Willems

ISBN: 978-1-4063-1229-4

YOUR PAL MO WILLEMS PRESENTS Leonardo the TERRIBLE MONSTER

ISBN: 978-1-4063-1215-7

Available from all good booksellers

www.walker.co.uk